Anonymous

Wilde's Summer Rose

Anatiposi

Anonymous

Wilde's Summer Rose

Reprint of the original.

1st Edition 2023 | ISBN: 978-3-38210-796-3

Anatiposi Verlag is an imprint of Outlook Verlagsgesellschaft mbH.

Verlag (Publisher): Outlook Verlag GmbH, Zeilweg 44, 60439 Frankfurt, Deutschland
Vertretungsberechtigt (Authorized to represent): E. Roepke, Zeilweg 44, 60439 Frankfurt, Deutschland
Druck (Print): Books on Demand GmbH, In de Tarpen 42, 22848 Norderstedt, Deutschland

WILDE'S SUMMER ROSE;

OR

THE

LAMENT OF THE CAPTIVE.

AN AUTHENTIC ACCOUNT OF THE ORIGIN, MYSTERY AND EXPLANATION OF
HON. R. H. WILDE's ALLEGED PLAGIARISM; BY

ANTHONY BARCLAY, ESQ.,

AND WITH HIS PERMISSION PUBLISHED BY

THE GEORGIA HISTORICAL SOCIETY.

SAVANNAH:
1871.

J. H. ESTILL, PRINTER, 111 BAY STREET.

PREFACE.

The GEORGIA HISTORICAL SOCIETY offer no apology for giving to the public this little volume. Apart from its intrinsic literary excellence, the matter is essentially *Georgian*, and as such claims the consideration of all who feel an interest in the literature as well as the history of this State.

It is true that neither of the persons, principally concerned in the transactions unfolded in the following pages, was born in Georgia. Mr. Wilde was a native of Ireland; Mr. Barclay was born a British subject, and remains so. The personal, literary and political history of the former is well known — his best days having been spent in the service of his adopted State. Mr. Barclay has been a resident of Savannah for more than fifty years; for, though occupied a long time as British Commissioner to direct the survey and to determine the boundary line from the river St. Lawrence to the Lake of the Woods, and afterwards as British Consul at New-York, he never failed to spend in Savannah some portion of each year, always most highly respected by her people for his many virtues and thorough classic culture.

In presenting this volume to the public, we feel that we furnish nothing new to those who, during Mr. Wilde's lifetime, read the same vindication of him, in the periodicals and newspapers of that day, and by the same friendly hand: But as the materials of the singular and interesting controversy, respecting Mr. Wilde's claim to the authorship of "The Summer Rose," lay scattered out of the reach of all except the industrious and favored few, it was believed that the collection and publication of these materials would not only subserve a literary purpose, but put into a condensed and authentic form, the origin, history and settlement of a controversy, which, at the time, excited deep interest, and which will hereafter and forever associate the names of the two principal persons connected with it.

The prefatory note of Mr. Barclay will show that the manuscript was not intended for the press; and the committee to whom the publication has been intrusted, take this method of returning to Mr. Barclay the thanks of the Society for his courteous permission to print it.

Besides the "narrative" itself and the papers embraced in it, the committee have taken the liberty to print other papers having an intimate relation to the primary affair.

Mr. Barclay's extract, (from Sir Charles Lyell's "Second Visit to the United States of North America,") may,

in one sense, be considered as the end of his contribution
to the "strange, eventful history"; but the committee
have deemed it proper to prefix to that extract the Review,
by APIS, in "The Southern Magazine," of a recent article which shows that the history of Mr. Wilde's alleged
plagiarism was not then fully understood.

THE COMMITTEE OF THE
GEORGIA HISTORICAL SOCIETY.

Savannah, March, 1871.

To the Hon. EDWARD J. HARDEN.

Savannah, Jan'y 26th, 1871.

My dear Sir:—

In compliance with your request, I have written for you the narrative, from alpha to omega, contained in this book, of the origin, mystery and *éclaircissement* of the translation into Greek of Mr. Wilde's touching verses, the LAMENT OF THE CAPTIVE. I could not have volunteered so small an affair for your acceptance.

With the greatest respect and regard,

I am,

My dear sir,

Your humble servant,

ANTH. BARCLAY.

The North American Magazine, No. XXVI., December, 1834, Vol. V., contains the following article:

PLAGIARISM.

Perhaps the history of letters, though it abounds with examples of singular coincidences, both in idea and expression, cannot present a more. extraordinary instance of plagiarism than that which it now becomes our duty, as a literary critic, to unfold. Ten or twelve years since, a little poem appeared, which was attributed to the Hon. R. H. Wilde, M. C. of Georgia; and it has probably. been republished through a hundred different media. The pathetic and tender feelings which it conveys, the exquisite truth of its images, and the melody of its verse, conspired to confer upon the reputed author of this little poem a fame which nothing so brief had previously ever secured even to the masters of

the lyre. We know not that the verses which
we publish below were ever actually asserted by
Mr. Wilde to be his original composition; but
opportunities, almost without number, have
occured to enable the honorable gentleman to
disclaim the title of author, and assume that,
merely, of translator. No such opportunity,
however, has been improved; and, until a recent
period, the cis-Atlantic world of letters were
pleased to award to Mr. Wilde, who, we have
heard, is an accomplished gentleman and scholar, the possession of a poetical genius peculiarly
felicitous. A weekly periodical* of New-York,
combining the laic with the clerical, during the
last summer published a communication which
claimed for an Irish Bard the original composition of the verses, which for so long a period had
been attributed to Mr. Wilde. " We wish," said
the editor of the print to which we refer, " we
wish to pluck the stolen laurels from the Honorable Plagiarist of Georgia, and replace those

---

* The Catholic Register and Diary.

offerings of the Irish muse on the literary shrines of Innisfallen, to which the poetic genius of O'Kelly, the esteemed and popular Bard of passion and patriotism, *originally* consecrated them." And the vain-glorious detector indulged in expressions of exulting folly with which we shall not stain these pages. His correspondent proceeded to assert, with true Hibernian impetuosity and confidence, that

" O'Kelly, the far-famed author of the ' Curse of Donerail,' who has sung wildly, though sweetly, of the unrivaled beauty and picturesque scenery of Killarney's Lake, and of the sublime grandeur of the Giants' Causeway, has published nothing possessing more pathetic beauty, in the same compass, than the following touching lines, ascribed by your good friend, Mr. Noah, of the Evening Star, to the Hon. Richard H. Wilde, of Georgia, and published a few days since, with some verbal alterations, in that paper. I, however, send you the original."

Now, the original verses, from which those of Mr. Wilde and those of the *far-famed* O'Kelly

2

are nothing but translations, were written by
Alcæus of Mitylene, one of the sweetest of all
the erotic bards of ancient Greece, twenty-four
hundred years ago!

The proof of this assertion we now proceed
to exhibit. Nothing but fragments of Alcæus'
works have descended to us, through the ruins of
revolutions, the convulsions of decaying empires,
and the barbarism and darkness of the middle
ages; but, one of his fragments, which we now
reprint side by side with a Latin translation, as
Mr. Wilde's version stands *vis à vis* with that of
O'Kelly, is, line by line and word by word, the
original, from which the little poem, that has
enjoyed and conferred so much reputation, is
derived. Some of the Greek phrases — such
is the exceedingly beautiful significance of the
original — it was impossible for any English
translator to convey with equal energy and
eloquence; but, by comparing the Greek with the
Latin, our prose * translation with the Greek,

---

* Too faulty to be worth inserting.

and the versions of Wilde and O'Kelly with all,
not a doubt can remain in the mind of any
scholar, that whatever renown this poem has
acquired, or may acquire, belongs exclusively
to the enthusiastic and inspired lover of Sappho.
We hope that Mr. Wilde has never assumed the
authorship of this poem; for we should indeed
regret to award to his knowledge what is due
only to his genius, and to confer upon his
ingenuity that which is due only to ingenuous-
ness. But, having now fulfilled the duty of a
literary critic, and for the first time unfolded
the whole subject before our men of letters, we
shall not shrink from the responsibility of the
exposition.

We have now presented this matter fairly
before the world; and it remains yet to learn
whether the verses of Mr. Wilde and O'Kelly
were translated from the Latin translation, or
derived directly from the original Greek.

From the Fragments of Alcæus.

1.

Τῷ ῥόδῳ θερινῷ ὁ βίος μου ὅμοιος,
Πρωῒ τῷ Φοίβῳ ἀναπτύσσοντι ἄνθος·
Πρὶν δὲ Νὺξ ἐπισκιάζῃ αὐτὸν μέλαινα,
Τὰ φύλλα ξηραίνεσθαι ὠχριῶντα πίπτει.

2.

Μείλιχος δὲ δρόσος ὑπὲρ ῥόδον ἀποστάζει,
Ἀποθνήσκοντι προφέρουσα ¹ἀντ' εὐοδμιῶν πότ-
  ημα,
Ἢ ὡς διαφθειρομένῳ ἐπὶ κάλλει δακρύουσα·
Τίς δ' αἶ, τίς αἶ, ἐπ' ἐμοὶ δακρύσει;

3.

Τοῖς φύλλοις τῆς ὀπώρας ὁ βίος μου ὅμοιος,
Αὔραις τρέμουσι καὶ εἰς γῆν ²ἀπορρέειν ἐτοίμοις·
Ἀλλοχροεῖ τὰ φύλλα, μόγις αὐτὰ συνέχει τὸ δέν-
  δρον,
Ἄστατα, εὔκλαστα, καὶ τελευτήσοντα.

4.

Τῶν φύλλων δὲ ἀρχομένων ἀποξηραίνεσθαι,
Ἐπὶ ταῖς ἀπογοναῖς στένει δένδρον χηρεῦσον,
Ἄνεμος μὲν κλαίει δένδρον ἄγλωττον·
Τίς δὲ μέ, τίς μέ ἀποθάνοντα κλαύσει;

ODE (ὁ βίος μου) ALCÆI.

Versio Latina.

1.

Rosæ æstivæ mea vita est similis,
Mane Phœbo explicanti florem;
Sed, priu͜squam illam Nox atra obumbret,
Folia, desiccanda, pallentia, cadunt:

2.

Blanda vero ros super rosam distillat,
Moribundæ adhibens pro fragantia potum;
Ceu, perituram pulchritudinem deflens:
Quis autem, eheu! quis, eheu! me deplorabit?

3.

Foliis autumni mea vita est similis,
Aura trementibus et in terram defluere paratis:
Colorem mutant folia; vix illa retinet arbor,
Instabilia, fragilia et decedenda:

4.

Incipientibus autem foliis exsiccari,
Sobolem gemet arbor vidua;
Arborem linguis orbatam lameutatur ventus:
Quis autem me, quis me moribundum deflebit?

5.

Τῷ βήματι ἐν ψάμμῳ ὁ βίος μου ὅμοιος,
Θνητῶν ἐντυπουμένῳ ποδῶν ἐπ' ἀκτῆς τῆς ¹Λεσ-
    βωῆς,
Οὐ πρὶν παρορμήσεται κλύδων, ἀσταϑὴς καὶ
    ὑγρός,
Ἤ ἴχνος εὐμετάβλητον ἀφανίσεται εἰς αἰῶνα.

6.

Ἀλλ᾽, ὡς ἴχνια βρότου ἀποτρίβεσϑαι λυπούμενα,
Τὰ κύματα συνεχὲς καταλαμβάνει πένϑος·
Ἐγὼ τῇ Σάπφοΐ μου τὸν ἔρωτα ζάων δέδωκα,
Τίς, εἰ μὴ Σάπφω, μέ μόνον, Μουσῶν καλλίστη,
    Θρηνήσει;

---

¹ Ἀντί, in return for.

² Ἀπορρέειν beautifully applied to the falling of hair
and the shedding of leaves.

³ The Island of Lesbos was the birth-place and resi-
dence of Alcæus and Sappho. That poet was the ardent
but unsuccessful admirer of the poetess. The last two
lines, with the reference to Lesbos, are the principal
grounds upon which this ode is ascribed to Alcæus.
The word μόνον refers to the life of celibacy to which
his love to her and her cruelty to him had destined
him, and which his fidelity determined him to close by
a corresponding death.

5.

Vestigio in arena mea vita est similis,
Hominis impresso pedibus super litus Lesboüm;
Non prius irruerit æstus inconstans et liquidus,
Quam vestigium mutabile evanescet in æternum.

6.

Sed, quasi vestigia humana delere mœrentes,
Undas perpetuus invadit luctus:
Quamdiu vivebam, Sapphoï meum dabam amorem;
Quis, nisi Sappho Musarum pulcherrima, me deso-
    latum lugebit?

THE SIMILE.

Written on the beautiful beach of Lehinch, in the county of Clare;
By PATRICK O'KELLY, the Irish Bard.

1.

My life is like the summer rose,
  That opens to the morning sky;
But, ere the shades of evening close,
  Is scattered on the ground — to die:

2.

But, on the rose's humble bed
  The sweetest dews of Night are shed;
As if she wept such waste to see;
  But who, alas! shall weep for me?

3.

My life is like the autumn leaf,
  That trembles in the moon's pale ray;
Its hold is frail — its date is brief;
  Restless — and soon to pass away:

4.

Yet, ere that leaf shall fall and fade,
  The parent tree shall mourn its shade;
The winds bewail the leafless tree:
  But who shall then bewail for me?

LINES,

By R. H. WILDE, Esq., of Augusta, Georgia.

1.

My life is like the *Summer Rose,
　That opens to the morning sky;
But, ere the shades of evening close,
　Is scattered on the ground—to die:

2.

But, on the rose s humble. bed
　The sweetest dews of Night are shed;
As if she wept such waste to see:
　But none shall weep a tear for me.

3.

My life is like the autumn leaf,
　That trembles in the moon's pale ray;
Its hold is frail, its date is brief,
　Restless, and soon to pass away:

4.

Yet, ere that leaf shall fall and fade,
　The parent tree shall mourn its shade;
The winds bewail the leafless tree;
　But none shall breathe a sigh for me.

---

* Summer Rose is the popular name of the species.

3

5.

My life is like the print, which feet
 Have left on Lehinch's desert strand;
Soon as the rising tide shall beat,
 The track will vanish from the sand:

6.

Yet, as if grieving to efface
 The vestige of the human race,
On that lone shore loud moans the sea:
 Who but the Nine shall moan for me?

5.

My life is like the print, which feet
  Have left on *Tampa's desert strand;
Soon as the rising tide shall beat,
  This track will vanish from the sand:

6.

Yet still, as grieving to efface
  All vestige of the human race,
On that lone shore loud moans the sea:
  But none shall e'er lament for me.

---

* Coast of Florida.

The North American Magazine, in its No. XXVIII., February, 1835, comes to the question whether the Greek ode was written in sport. On this point the writer of that article asks (p. 272): "Would any man, (if the deed were possible to any but a Porson,) devote himself to the protracted toil necessary for such a task of translating Mr. Wilde's verses into Greek, and prove himself, by *new images,** quite equal to his *original*, merely for the pleasure of *humbugging* the literary world?"

The same number of the North American

---

* Here the Magazine has a note, as follows: "Let us suppose for a moment that this unfortunate Greek ode is a translation of Mr. Wilde's verses: it follows, then, that the translator blundered in his business, and produced from his own brain more poetry than he found; for where, in Mr. W.'s poem, shall we find that beautiful metaphor, 'the voiceless tree among its children moans'? — and where shall we find the name of Sappho, the most beautiful of the Muses, or any reference to the solitude of the lyrist? There are also other words and lines in the Greek as pregnant with poetry as any in Mr. Wilde's verses. The alleged *hoaxer* must have had an infinite regard for the *hoaxed*, thus to augment the attractions of this poem by additions of his own."

Magazine, at page 273, quotes from the Literary and Catholic Sentinel, of Boston, under date January 3d, 1835, as follows: "The next packet from Liverpool arriving at New-York will, in all probability, bring Mr. O'Kelly's answer, which shall, we predict, not only establish irrefutably the claim of Mr. O'Kelly of being the original *translator from the Greek of Alcæus*, but fasten on Mr. Wilde the plagiarist's badge.   As soon as Mr. O'Kelly's letter arrives, we will give* it to our readers, with appropriate comments."

---

* It has not yet been given—in January, 1871.

ORIGIN OF THE GREEK ODE.

For four months after the first appearance of
the Greek ode, it was a subject of astonishment,
wonder, faith, and but little doubt of its genu-
ineness. The only matter for wonder in the
mind of one person was, that it should be a
question of general interest where it was heard
of, for more than a few days. As the Mytilene
in which it was produced is now well known,
the following narrative may be amusing to you,
being a brief account of its origin; of the means
adopted to bring it into notice; and of the
efforts made to obtain the veritable Odes of
Alcæus, among which it was fully expected that
it would be found. To proceed, then, with those
details.

The Greek lines, called Ode, were not intended to go before the public, in print. Such
an idea never entered the mind of the writer of
them, when they were being composed. They
were first designed exclusively for a few friends,
who, one happy sultry Wednesday evening in

the month of August, 1834, had accidentally met at the house, in Savannah, of GRÆCULUS, when one of their topics of conversation was the then recent charge brought against Mr. Wilde, of his plagiarism of "My life is like the summer rose," etc., from the so-styled Irish bard, O'KELLY. One of the party ascribed Mr. Wilde's pretty verses to a Greek original. When the visitors had dispersed, GRÆCULUS observed to one of his household who had been present: "Well, to-morrow I shall be at leisure; I will translate Mr. Wilde's verses into Greek, and when that simple man sees the Greek and is told that the ideas throughout are almost identical, he will put it down as clear proof of his correct information in classic literature." Thus originated the idea of a Greek translation.

When, on the next morning, Thursday, that vulgar necessity of breakfast was disposed of, GRÆCULUS retired to his library and began at Τῷ ῥόδῳ θερινῷ. Before the hour for dinner had arrived, GRÆCULUS sought the partner of his sympathies, and said to her, "It is done:

while I have been writing the Greek, I have
come to the belief that it may puzzle some persons of more learning than the one for whom it
was first intended; and I shall try it." So, on
the succeeding day, Friday, he wrote a translation of his Greek into Latin, which rendered
the meaning of the Greek intelligible to many
who could not read that language. He added
three short notes, merely to produce a verisimil-
itude to the work of a scholiast: he prepared the
verses in form as designed to be issued by him
—the Greek on one page, and the Latin corresponding therewith on the opposite page—stanza
by stanza—also the lines ascribed to O'Kelly,
and those of Mr. Wilde, arranged in similar
manner, on opposite pages, as set forth in this
book. The draft of the manuscript was thus
complete. He determined that a fair copy of it
should, on the following day, be put into such a
channel as would be sure to float it about on a
good current of curiosity; but his own hand-
writing was not to appear. A youth in his own
family wrote the Greek characters beautifully,

and was to be depended upon for reticence; and he gave him notice to repair to the library, the next morning, for the purpose of copying the whole. On Saturday he was there, and finished all in good style. GRÆCULUS then fixed on an excellent, cheerful friend, with whom he was intimate—the pastor of a church in Savannah—who had intelligence, inquisitiveness, and critical taste in literary matters, and would value the stray paper, whether genuine or counterfeit, as a person into whose possession the paper should be directed. To effect that object, a letter was written to him by one Terence Doyle, enclosing the Greek lines and their appurtenances, as just found by him, which he represented to be unintelligible to him; but he doubted not that the pastor in his great learning would understand to what they related, and know what disposition to make of them.

The letter was written in a strange hand. The packet was left, that evening, at the parsonage, by a person attired as Terence Doyle.

On Monday, when GRÆCULUS was at dinner,

4

having three or four friends to give enjoyment
to his meal, a servant announced: "The Rev-
erend Mr.—— wishes to see you in the hall."
GRÆCULUS thought, "Now comes the charge,"
and immediately went out to the pastor, and
begged him to join his guests at the dinner-table.
"No, no," he said; "stop a moment;" and draw-
ing out a packet, he opened it at the Greek ode,
and handed it to GRÆCULUS, saying: "There! is
not that strange?" GRÆCULUS fixed his eyes
on the first lines of the ode; continued so for a
few moments as if reading them; and then, look-
ing the parson in the face, remarked to him:
"Why, those lines are identical in thought and
in all the parts of speech with Mr. Wilde's pretty verses, 'My life is like the summer rose,'
called Lament of the Captive." "Is it not extraordinary?", he said. GRÆCULUS, whose con-
science had made a coward of him, perceived
that he was unsuspected, and took courage. The
parson proceeded: "Have you a copy of Alcæus?" GRÆCULUS answered that commenta-
tors differed about the fragments ascribed to

him ; that he had a volume of Greek odes by various authors, but that he did not remember that this one was in it; that he would get the book for him, however, before he went away. The parson added: "Well, I have written to Petigru to search the Charleston Library for Alcæus, and to send it to me if he find it." They then joined the company at the dinner-table, and the parson's wonderful possession became the topic of conversation.

The desired volume was not found in the Charleston Library. Terence Doyle's manu-script was submitted to the knowing ones in Savannah, by whom several copies of it were made. One of them was sent to the President of the College at Athens, Georgia, where, if any-where, spuriousness should have been detected. He was reported to have pronounced the Greek to be pure and ancient, but he could not say whether it was of Alcæus or not, as his odes were not in the library there. Curiosity about it continued to exist in Savannah for some time.

In November, 1834, when GRÆCULUS had

ceased to think of the matter, he removed with his family to reside in New-York, believing that his foundling would never be heard of again. How great was his surprise, then, to receive on the 9th of January, 1835, in that city, a letter dated Washington, January 7th, 1835, from Mr. Wilde, making inquiry about the authorship of the Greek ode, of the publication of which in print GRÆCULUS was not then informed.

Thereupon ensued the *dénouement* of the affair, as contained in an article published in a weekly literary paper of that time — The New-York Mirror of February 28th, 1835 — of which the following is a copy.

NOTE.—Before proceeding with that copy, it is pleasant to relate that the dear, good, amiable pastor never, after the *dénouement* of the mystery, met GRÆCULUS, without asking him, with a smile, whether he had another Greek ode for him yet.

NEW-YORK MIRROR, FEBRUARY 28, 1835.

MY LIFE IS LIKE A SUMMER ROSE.

HON. MR. WILDE, O'KELLY, AND ALCÆUS.

Few of our readers, we imagine, are ignorant of the various claims which have been lately brought forward, in the periodicals and newspapers, to the authorship of the beautiful lines, beginning, "My life is like the summer rose," which have been some twenty years before the public as the acknowledged, and until lately the unquestioned, production of Richard Henry Wilde, a distinguished representative in Congress from the State of Georgia.

After this long acquiescence in the claims of that gentleman, his title has lately been contested, first by a friend of O'Kelly, an Irish bard, and secondly by critics appearing in behalf of no less a personage than Alcæus, a Greek lyrical poet who flourished about six hundred years before the Christian era. In the one case, Mr. Wilde is charged with downright plagiarism ; in the other, with palming upon the world a translation from the Greek as an original composition of his own. Both of these charges are equally derogatory to his character as a man of honor; and, however indifferent himself and his friends may be to his reputation as a poet, it was hardly expected that they would sit quiet under imputations that so nearly affect his reputation for candor and veracity. As one among his many friends and admirers, we have taken the pains to make a thorough examination into these respective claims, and now lay the result before our readers — beginning with a brief detail of the origin of the lines in question, the circumstances under which they were written, and the manner of their coming before the public. We shall avail ourselves, for this purpose, of Mr. Wilde's own language in a letter to an intimate friend in this city:

"The lines in question, you will perceive, were originally intended as part of a longer poem. My brother, the late James Wilde, was an officer of the United States army, and held a subaltern rank in the expedition of Colonel

John Williams against the Seminole Indians
of Florida, which first broke up their towns
and stopped their atrocities. When James
returned, he amused my mother, then alive,
my sisters and myself, with descriptions of the
orange - groves and transparent lakes, the
beauty of the St. John's river and of the woods
and swamps of Florida, a kind of fairy land —
of which we then knew little except from Bar-
tram's ecstacies — interspersed with anecdotes
of his campaign and companions. As he had
some taste himself, I used to laugh and tell him
I 'd immortalize his exploits in an epic. Some
stanzas were accordingly written for the amusement of the family at our meetings. That, alas!
was destined never to take place. He was
killed in a duel. His violent and melancholy
death put an end to my poem ; the third stanza
of the first fragment, which alludes to his fate,
being all that was written afterwards. The
verses, particularly the 'Lament of the Captive,' were read by the family and some intimate acquaintances; among the rest, the present

Secretary of State,* and a gentleman then a student of medicine, now a distinguished physician in Philadelphia. The latter, after much importunity, procured from me, for a lady in that city, a copy of 'My life is like the summer rose,' with an injunction against publicity, which the lady herself did not violate; but a musical composer, to whom she gave the words for the purpose of setting them, did; and they appeared, I think, first in 1815 or 1816, with my name and addition at full length, to my no small annoyance. Still, I never avowed them; and though continually republished in the newspapers with my name, and a poetical reply, I maintained that newspapers were no authority, and refused to answer further. I resisted even the inclination to say that there was no personal allusion in the lines—no small effort of self-control, considering how vexatiously certain the contrary assumption appeared."

----

* Mr. Forsyth.

The following are fragments of the poem alluded to in the foregoing statement; from which it will appear how naturally the lines claimed for O'Kelly and Alcæus incorporate themselves with the subject-matter preceding them. They will also serve to show, what indeed Mr. Wilde has proved in many other instances, that if he is not the author of the verses claimed by O'Kelly, he is capable of writing others quite as good:

FRAGMENT I.

[The first and second stanzas of this Fragment in the New-York Mirror, consisting of nine lines each, are here omitted, having been introduced merely to show Mr. Wilde's poetic talent; but the third stanza, being an interesting allusion to his brother's death, is as follows:]

I too had once a brother; he was there
Among the foremost, bravest of the brave;
To him this lay was framed with fruitless care;
Sisters for him the sigh in secret gave;

5

For him a mother poured the fervent prayer.
But sigh or prayer availeth not to save
A generous victim in a villain's snare:
He found a bloody but inglorious grave,
And never nobler heart was racked by baser glaive.

[Fragment II., a long one, and Fragment
III., are here omitted for the same reasons
as were the two stanzas of Fragment I.]

FRAGMENT IV.

'T is many moons ago; a' long, long time
Since first upon this shore a white man trod.
From the great water to the mountain clime,
This was our home; 't was given us by the God
That gave you yours. Love ye your native sod?
So did our fathers too, for they were men:
They fought to guard it, for their hearts were brave;
And long they fought! We were a people then,
This was our country; it is now our grave:
Would I had never lived, or died this land to save!

When first ye came, your numbers were but few,
Our nation many as the leaves or sand:
Hungry and tired ye were; we pitied you,
We called you brothers; took you by the hand;
But soon we found ye came to spoil the land:

We quarreled, and your countrymen we slew,
Till one alone of all remained behind ;
Among the false he only had been true,
And much we loved this man of single mind,
And ever while he lived to him were kind.

He loved us too, and taught us many things,
And much we strove the stranger's heart to glad ;
But to its kindred still the spirit clings,
And therefore was his soul forever sad ;
Nor other wish or joy the lone one had,
Save on the solitary shore to roam,
Or sit and gaze for hours upon the deep
That rolled between him and his native home ;
And when he thought none marked him, he would
      weep,
Or sing this song of woe which still our maidens
      keep :

LAMENT OF THE CAPTIVE.

My life is like the summer rose,
    That opens to the morning sky;
And ere the shades of evening close,
    Is scattered on the ground — to die:

Yet, on that rose's humble bed
　　The softest dews of Night are shed;
As if she wept such waste to see:
　　But none shall drop a tear for me!

My life is like the autumn leaf,
　　That trembles in the moon's pale ray;
Its hold is frail, its date is · brief —
　　Restless, and soon to pass away:
Yet, when that leaf shall fall and fade,
　　The parent tree will mourn its shade;
The wind bewail the leafless tree:
　　But none shall breathe a sigh for me!

My life is like the print, which feet
　　Have left on Tampa's desert strand;
Soon as the rising tide shall beat,
　　Their track will vanish from the sand:
Yet, as if grieving to efface
　　All vestige of the human race,
On that lone shore loud moans the sea:
　　But none shall thus lament for me!

The first part of the fourth Fragment is the
supposed indignant address of a savage chief
to one of the American officers: the latter

part, the lament of a Spanish captive, the last survivor of Panfilo de Narvaez's ill-fated expedition. See Garcilasso de la Vega — Historia de la Florida — for an account of the sufferings of Juan Ortiz Tom: 1, cap: XVII.

With regard to the claim of O'Kelly, the first circumstance that will strike the reader is its having remained in abeyance for such a long period ; and that it is now presented, for the first time, after a lapse of some twenty years of entire oblivion. This is the more remarkable, from the fact that the lines in question were published upwards of ten years ago, in a selection of American poems called "The Columbian Lyre," printed at Glasgow, in Scotland, and afterwards copied in various ways both in England and Ireland. Still, no claim was advanced in behalf of the Irish bard, whose name is now for the first time brought forward for the purpose of plucking the wreath which Mr. Wilde has so long worn without a rival. On subsequent inquiry, we learn that O'Kelly is a sort of wandering bard, whose education and habits render it next to impossible that he should have written verses so remarkable for their delicate sentiment and polished elegance. They distinctly iudicate a mind of rich cultivation, purified by the habitual indulgence of sentiments which could hardly be felt, and certainly not so expressed, by any but a person of the highest refinement of mind. The first stanzas of the piece, in our opinion, furnish other conclusive evidence against the claim of O'Kelly. The allusion to the rose —

"That opens to the morning sky,
And, ere the shades of evening close,
Is scattered on the ground — to die "—

could only apply, even with poetical justice, to the Florida rose, which, as Mr. Wilde states in the note, "opens, fades, and perishes during the summer in less than twelve hours." It would be false and forced in relation to any other species of rose, and could only naturally present itself to the imagination of a southern poet, who alone would be likely to be familiar with its touching poetical associations. The probability of its occurring to an Irish bard of the character of O'Kelly, is so remote as in our opinion to amount to a complete bar to his pretensions. There are many other reasons why we discard the claim of O'Kelly entirely. In the first instance, he was put forth as the original author ;. but when the Fragment of the Greek poet was placed before the public in such an imposing form, and the original Greek produced, the same authority, which had challenged the authorship for O'Kelly, then claimed the verses as a translation, and charged Mr. Wilde with copying that. Surely, these inconsistencies, and this entire change of ground, indicate somewhat distinctly that the counsel for O'Kelly has not thoroughly studied his case, and is not quite so well acquainted with the facts as he would wish to appear. As yet, the claim of O'Kelly rests, as we believe — for we have seen no other — on the authority of an anonymous writer in "The New-York Weekly Register and Catholic Diary", of the ninth of

August, 1834. That our readers may have all proof before them, we subjoin the letter of the unknown correspondent, the comments of the editor, and the verses claimed by O'Kelly. Both the letter and the comments are equally distinguished by arrogant discourtesy.

"We cheerfully give insertion to the following communication from our respected correspondent in Albany, as we wish to pluck the stolen laurels from the honorable plagiarist of Georgia, and replace those offerings of the Irish muse on the literary shrine of Innisfallen, to which the poetic genius, O'Kelly, the esteemed and popular bard of passion and patriotism, originally consecrated them. The white feathers of the singing Swan of Killarney, thanks to the detection of our correspondent, have not been long suffered to remain as felonious ornaments in the black wings of the Georgian Gander."

"*To the Editor of the Register and Diary :*
That the daw may not strut his brief hour in

the borrowed plumage of the eagle, I would beg leave to call your attention to the following :

'O'Kelly, the far-famed author of the Curse of Doneraile', who has sung wildly, though sweetly, of the unrivaled beauty and picturesque scenery of Killarney's lake, and of the sublime grandeur of the Giants' Causeway, has published nothing possessing more pathetic beauty, in the same compass, than the following touching lines ascribed by your good friend, Mr. Noah of the 'Evening Star', to the honorable Richard Henry Wilde, of Georgia, and ,published a few days since, with some verbal alterations, in that paper. I, however, send you the original, together with the answer by our talented young countryman, Mr. J. O'Leary, of Cork; by your publishing which, in the 'Register', together with a few prefatory remarks of your own, I shall feel much indebted to you. Hoping that our common yet dear country may not be robbed of her just meed of poetic fame, nor a plagiarist receive the applause more

6

justly due to one who feels proud of having merited a portion of Erin's ancient bardic lore,

I remain yours, respectfully,

J. C. P.

ALBANY, July 8th, 1834.

THE SIMILE.

Written on the beautiful beach of Lehinch, in the county of Clare;
By PATRICK O'KELLY, the Irish Bard."

[The verses here introduced in the New-York Mirror, as O'Kelly's, correspond, *verbatim*, with those inserted at pp. 12–14 of this manuscript (see printed pages 16–18), as claimed by O'Kelly. The whole is therefore here omitted.]

We appeal to the candor of our readers, to say whether the mere naked assertion of an anonymous writer, couched in such language as this, and backed simply by a copy of the "original" verses of O'Kelly, as he is pleased to call them, without explaining from what source they are derived, or producing one single proof of their authenticity; whether

such flimsy assertions as these, sanctioned by
no name, and supported by no authority whatever, ought to weigh for a moment against
twenty years of quiet acquiescence in the claim
of Mr. Wilde. Perhaps no poem, ever written
in this country, has had a more extensive cir-
culation in newspapers and periodicals; and
yet now, for the first time, it is seen and rec-
ognized by the anonymous writer, and claimed
for the far-famed author of the "Curse of Doneraile". By the way, the answer of Mr. J.
O'Leary, of Cork, is not given in the Diary.
Was it *verbatim* with the answer to these lines
by a lady of Baltimore, and therefore with-
held from a principle of gallantry? Or did the
editor suspect that two plagiarisms would be
rather too much for the public credulity? Fur-
thermore, as yet the claim of O'Kelly remains
entirely unsupported by any testimony, except
the mere assertion of a friend; although that
friend has been repeatedly challenged to produce either direct or circumstantial evidence
of the plagiarism. The charge made in one

form is reiterated in another; but no proof
whatever adduced, and no explanation of the
delay in making this serious attack on the veracity and honor of a gentleman. Assuredly,
if O'Kelly is the author of the lines in question,
as his friends appear so zealous in his behalf,
they might ere this have procured from some
quarter or other something like demonstrative
proof in the shape of O'Kelly's works, or his
own declaration — for we believe he is still
living — or the testimony of some responsible
person, who might at least offer circumstantial,
if not direct, evidence in behalf of his claim.
Nothing, however, of this kind has been procured to support a pretension which is rendered
equally frivolous and improbable, as well by the
whole train of circumstances attending it as by
that internal evidence which to persons of taste
and judgment is the most infallible of all testimony. Taking this into consideration, we do
not hesitate to pronounce the charge against
Mr. Wilde to be entirely unsupported by any
authority that should, in the slightest degree,

weigh against the character and veracity of that gentleman.

We now come to the formidable claim of the old Greek poet, which however is easily put to sleep. Notwithstanding the testimony of the editor of the North American Magazine, that the Fragment he published is a genuine fragment which has hitherto escaped all the researches of the learned, we think we could easily prove that, though pure Greek, it is neither Alcaic Greek, nor intended by the author for Greek poetry, or any other kind of poetry. It is thus analyzed by a young gentleman, a native of Philadelphia, whose communication we have now before us, and would insert at length, had we room or were it necessary to our purpose. It was written immediately after the appearance of the Greek Ode, but miscarried in the transmission, and only came to hand lately. "That it is not the production of an ancient Greek poet, is conclusively proved by the absence of the dialects which, as it were, incrust the Greek poetry of

the age of Alcæus. Few, very few, modern
hands, it is believed, can manage these, and
the able but discreet author of the 'Fragment'
has wisely avoided them. The whole production is pure and well-arranged Greek, but is
very different from the Greek of the poets of
the age to which it is referred. But, in fact,
it is not poetry at all. The piece, though very
ingeniously managed, is evidently prosaic. The
fragments of Alcæus are accessible to perhaps
few; but let those to whom they are not
so turn to the fragment of Simonides, a poet
nearly contemporary with Alcæus, as given
by Warton in Hawkesworth's Adventurer,
number eighty-nine, and make the comparison.
The difference is as obvious as between the
poetry of Spenser and the prose of Goldsmith.
To this we might add what every scholar knows,
or ought to know before he pretends to be a
critic in Greek poetry, that Alcæus wrote uni-
formly in one measure peculiar to himself, and
hence called the Alcaic. The pure fragment
brought forward by the 'North American Mag-

azine', is assuredly no more Alcaic than the English translation of that gentleman's true version of the original."

To settle the question, however, beyond all controversy, we give the following letters. From that of Mr. Barclay, it will be seen that the Fragment in question, from which some twenty years ago Mr. Wilde translated his fine lines, was written a few months since, in Savannah, by a gentleman now resident in this city, with the sole view to his own amusement and that of a few private friends. That it found its way to the public, and became the foundation of a charge against Mr. Wilde far more formidable than the claim of the Irish pretender, was entirely contrary to his wishes or expectations, and is equally a subject of regret. Few among the scholars of modern date could probably have achieved this harmless pleasantry; and we feel assured that none could have been more pained and surprised at learning its ultimate destination and consequences.

WASHINGTON, 7th January, 1835.

Dear Sir:

Relying on our past acquaintance, and your known urbanity, to pardon the liberty I take, permit me to say, without farther preface, that circumstances, which it is unnecessary to detail, concur in pointing you out as the author of a translation, into Greek, of some fugitive verses long attributed to, but only recently avowed by, me. If you are, I am sure the task was executed only to amuse the leisure hours of a gentleman and scholar, or at most for the sport it might afford you to mystify the learned. In the latter, you have been so eminently success-ful, if the work is yours, that a result has been produced, the reverse no doubt of your inten-tion, so far as respects myself. I have been stigmatized with plagiarism, and compelled, such was the importance some of my friends attached to the charge, to deny it in person. Since then, an article in the Georgian, of the twenty-seventh of December, goes far to excul-pate me from the pillage of Alcæus; and excel-

lent reasons have been given, by Greek scholars, to show the piece is modern. Nevertheless,
as I have been compelled to do penance, pub-
licly, in sheets once white, for this sin of my
youth, it would relieve me somewhat, since I
must acknowledge the foundling, to have no
dispute about the paternity. The Greek fragment is so well executed as to deceive many
of some pretensions to scholarship. I am
therefore desirous of obtaining for publication,
in such form as you choose, your avowal of the
authorship; or, if you prefer it, your simple
authority for the fact. If I am wrong in ascrib-
ing it to you, your acquaintance with the society of Savannah will perhaps enable you to
inform me to whom I should address myself.

Permit me to renew the assurance of the
high respect and regard with which I have
the honor to be, dear sir,

Your obedient servant,

RICHARD HENRY WILDE.

To ANTHONY BARCLAY, Esq.,

of Savannah —

now in New-York. 7

NEW-YORK, January 24th, 1835.

My Dear Sir :

I was not apprised, when I addressed you on the 9th instant, nor for some days after, that my prose translation, into Greek, of your beautiful ode, beginning

"My life is like the summer rose,"

had been published ; otherwise, I could not at that short time have passed over the circumstance in utter silence. It was written for individual amusement with exclusively half a dozen acquaintance in Savannah, and without the slightest intention of its going further. This assertion will account for the abundant defects, and they will vouch for its truth. I as little believed that any credit, beyond the hour of surprise among my acquaintance before mentioned, would be awarded to my crude translation as I apprehended that any doubt could be created concerning the originality of your finished production. Metre and prosodiacal quantity were designedly disregarded ;

and this fact was sufficient to detect the spuriousness of the attempt, and to vindicate me
from any suspicion of expecting a successful de-
ception. If that effect has in any degree been
brought about, I must repeat, (to employ your
language,) that a result has been produced, the
reverse of my intention as far as regards your-
self, from whose brow I have had good reason
to believe, for the last sixteen years or more,
that modesty alone detained the poetic wreath.
I cannot say how extremely I regret the indis-
creet publication. Truly reluctant, however,
as I am, to come before the public, I shall feel
strong inducement to be resigned, if the translator succeed in dragging his author out of con-
cealment, and that event contribute to strip all
masks and to bestow honor where honor is due.

With great truth and regard, I am

Your faithful servant,

ANTHONY BARCLAY.

Hon. RICHARD HENRY WILDE, M. C.,
Washington, D. C.

Note by the Committee of the Georgia Historical Society.—In giving place to the following Review, we beg to call attention to the fact that the industrious, learned, and usually correct Mr. Allibone, in the third volume of his "Critical Dictionary," page 2718, in publishing the reviewed "note" of Mr. Stillé, except the first sentence, adds: "We are not a little amazed at the alleged skepticism of this plain-spoken 'Oxford scholar.'"

From "The Southern Magazine," March, 1871.

REVIEWS.

Proceedings of the American Philosophical Society, held at Philadelphia, for promoting Useful Knowledge.   Vol. XI.

A pamphlet, whose title is given above, has recently been brought to our notice. It contains, among other contributions, an article headed " Obituary Notice of Horace Binney, Jr., by Charles J. Stillé." It is written in a fervent spirit, as if stimulated by the author's grateful recollection of the deceased as the gentle and firm Christian, the accomplished scholar, and the acceptable associate of all refined and good men. He sets forth Mr. Binney's purity and goodness; the powerful influence of his character upon those around him; his extreme modesty, and utter aversion to display or ostentation of any kind; his genuine scholarly instincts; his love of the familiar intercourse of the wise, the true, and the good; his familiarity with ancient literature and ancient history; the classical spirit, with which he was imbued, forming the basis of all his canons of taste and criticism; his character as a conservative churchman, with a devout and earnest spirit upholding a high standard of Christian life and duty; his maintaining his convictions with courage and constancy; his unassuming manner; his innate sense of courtesy, preserving him from the slightest taint of arrogance;—with a heart as simple as a child's and as tender as a woman's; his life was nurtured and strengthened by the two great principles out of which all true excellence springs—trust in God and devotion to duty.

No doubt Mr. Binney not only consulted his taste, but measured his capacity, in the course of life which he adopted. The obituary is a well-written, neat, and pleasing memorial.

Our author has made mention of Mr. Binney's proficiency in the ancient Greek language. In connection with this point, our memory of a literary *jeu d'esprit*, which was perpetrated in Savannah so long ago as the year 1834, affecting, (as it was thought,) the candor and reputation of an honorable, accomplished gentleman of Georgia, and calling forth opinions and criticisms of both scholars and pretenders, North and South, in the United States, has lately been revived by an incidental reference to it in a note at page 375 of the pamphlet under consideration, in which the writer remarks, as follows :

"The following anecdote will illustrate Mr. Binney's familiarity with the Greek style : Mr. Richard Henry Wilde, once a member of Congress from Georgia, and an accomplished scholar, had written some beautiful verses, beginning, 'My life is like the summer rose,' etc., which, being published in the newspapers, became widely known. Some time after, Mr. Wilde was surprised to find in a Georgia newspaper a Greek ode purporting to have been written by Alcæus, an early Eolian poet of somewhat obscure fame, and it was claimed that Mr. Wilde's verses were simply a translation of this ode; the ideas in both being almost identical. As Mr. Wilde had never heard of Alcæus, he was much puzzled to account for this resemblance of the two poems. At the suggestion of a friend, the Greek ode was sent to Mr. Binney, for examination and criticism. He at once, much to the relief of Mr. Wilde, pronounced it a forgery, pointing out wherein its style differed from that of classical Greek. It turned out, afterwards, that the ode in question had been written by an Oxford scholar, on a wager that no one in that university was sufficiently familiar with the style of the early Greek poets to detect the counterfeit. To carry out this scheme, he had translated Mr. Wilde's verses into Greek."

Mr. Stillé has made some singular mistakes,

we think, in his narrative respecting the Greek translation of the graceful verses of the Hon. R. H. Wilde; and several matters, which he states as facts, are errors. The Greek ode, represented to be a fragment of Alcæus, was never found in a Georgia newspaper, as stated by Mr. Stillé. It first made its appearance in Georgia and elsewhere, in August, 1834, by means of manuscript copies. It was printed, for the first time, in the *North American Magazine* of December, 1834, published in Philadelphia, which charged Mr. Wilde with plagiarism by translation from the Greek.

The prevailing and growing indifference, or aversion even, in the United States, to derivative orthography, in deference to the unlearned majority, appears to have affected the author of the obituary — in writing *Eolian* instead of *Æolian*. Some of his learned brothers of the American Philosophical Society ought to have been good-natured enough to recommend him to adhere, in that case, to literary exactness; also to have hinted to him that the "poet of

somewhat obscure fame", as he describes Alcæus, who lived 600 years B. C., was as well
known in character as was Homer, Sophocles,
Euripides, Anacreon. His poetical productions
are reported by ancient writers to have been
many; and they were of such finished beauty
that the great Roman rhetorician and writer,
Quintilian, who lived in the first century of the
Christian era, wrote on him a splendid eulogium.
The extant fragments of Alcæus may be found
in Athenæus. Men may become as familiar
with authors, whose works they have never
seen, as with countries which they have never
visited. The writer of the obituary has ad-
mitted that Mr. Wilde was "an accomplished
scholar"; yet, a few lines farther on, he says
of him, that he "had never heard of Alcæus."
He unquestionably deserved the former character, being an ornament to the best society; and
he was doubtless as well acquainted with the
fame of Alcæus, as all other men of learning
who are not exclusively devoted to ancient

8

literature.   He never considered the Greek
poet to be "of obscure fame."

Our author remarks, that, when the Greek
ode was referred to Mr. Binney, he at once pronounced it a forgery; pointing out wherein its
style differed from that of classical Greek.
Now, we happened to be a contemporary of
Mr. Wilde, and corresponded with him in
regard to this very subject.   He wrote, in January, 1835, that it had been analyzed by a
young gentleman, a native of Philadelphia,
meaning (no doubt) Mr. Horace Binney, Jr.,
who stated : "that it is not the production of
an ancient Greek poet, is conclusively proved
by the absence of the dialects which, as it were,
incrust the Greek poetry of the age of Alcæus.
Few, very few, modern hands, it is believed,
can manage these ; and the able but discreet
author of the 'Fragment' [as the Greek was
termed] has wisely avoided them.   The whole
production is pure and well-arranged Greek."
The above statement found its way into print
in a *New-York Mirror*, a weekly paper of enter-

taining literature, of February, 1835. How different it is from the remark of the writer of the obituary, that Mr. Binney "pointed out wherein its style differed from that of classical Greek," to wit, "the whole production is pure and well-arranged Greek."

The most amusing part of our author's note to his obituary is the concluding paragraph, in which he says : "It turned out afterwards that the ode in question had been written by an Oxford scholar, on a wager that no one in that University was sufficiently familiar with the style of the early Greek poets to detect the counterfeit. To carry out this scheme, he had translated Mr. Wilde's verses into Greek." The so-called Oxford scholar, with whom we have been pretty well acquainted, was in Savannah when he wrote the Greek in question, (at a time when Mr. Wilde was absurdly charged with plagiarism of his verses from the Irish bard, O'Kelly,) to amuse himself by testing the scholarship and credulity of a few friends in that place, whom he had heard discussing the matter. He is now living in Georgia. He designedly made no attempt at dialect or metre, though he might have done both with success; but he depended on the rhythm and melody of his lines to cause it to be taken for granted that they were proso-diacal—"numerisque fertur *lege solutis*";—and in this he was not disappointed, for even Mr. Binney is not reported to have remarked upon the fact that there was no metre in the ode; and although it is said in the note that he often read the Greek Testament, it did not require a very intimate acquaintance with prosody to do that. As the Alcaic measure, introduced by Alcæus, from whom it takes its name, is but little known, perhaps he passed the ode as such. GRÆCULUS, in his jocose composition, anticipated this as likely with some of its critics. He never made the wager spoken of. There were a thousand men in Oxford, he well knew, who would instantly have detected the joke, and would not have left it for Mr. Binney to discover that there was no Æolic (or Alcaic) brogue in its dialect —but that "it is pure Greek," Attic. The writer of it himself informed his friend, Mr. Wilde, that he was the author of it, as soon as he heard of its publication, about the 9th of January, 1835; and he received Mr. Wilde's thanks expressed in beautiful and playful terms.

It is as desirable in literary as in forensic matters to arrive at facts. On this account these observations are written.

APIS.

Savannah, Jan. 25th, 1871.

Sir CHARLES LYELL, the well-known geologist, in his book called "A Second Visit to the United States of North America," speaking of Mr. Wilde, gives the following narrative: "He is well known in the literary world as the author of a work on the 'Love and Madness of Tasso,' published in 1842; and perhaps still more generally by some beautiful lines, beginning, 'My life is like the summer rose,' which are usually supposed to have derived their tone of touching melancholy from his grief at the sudden death of a brother; and soon after of a mother, who

never recovered the shock of her son's death.
As there had been so much controversy about
this short poem, we asked Mr. Wilde to relate
to us its true history, which is curious. He
had been one of a party at Savannah when the
question was raised whether a certain professor
of the University of Georgia understood Greek;
on which, one of his companions undertook to
translate Mr. Wilde's verses, called 'The Com-
plaint of the Captive,' into Greek prose, so
arranged as to appear like verse, and then see
if he could pass it off on the professor as a
fragment of Alcæus. The trick succeeded; although the professor said that, not having the
works of Alcæus at hand, he could not feel
sure that the poem was really his. It was then
sent, without the knowledge of Mr. Wilde or his
friends, to a periodical at New-York, and published as a fragment from Alcæus, and the Sen-
ator from Georgia was vehemently attacked by
his political opponents, for having passed off a
translation from the Greek as an original composition of his own.

Soon after this affair, Captain Basil Hall mentioned, in his 'Schloss Hainfeld,' (chap. 10,) that
the Countess Purgstall had read the lines to
him, and would not tell him who was the
author; but he had little doubt that she had
written them herself. The verses had become
so popular that they were set to music; and the
name of Tampa, a desolate sea-beach on the
coast of Florida, was changed into Tempe, the
loveliest of the wooded valleys of Greece, in
the concluding stanza :—

> ' My life is like the prints, which feet
>   Have left on Tampa's desert strand;
> Soon as the rising tide shall beat,
>   All trace will vanish from the sand:
> Yet, as if grieving to efface
>   All vestige of the human race,
> On that lone shore loud moans the sea;
>   But none, alas! shall mourn for me.'

In the countess' version, Zara has been substi-
tuted for Tampa."

[As a part of the history of the times, we

print the following from the Savannah Georgian, of 27th December, 1834, written by Dr.
R. D. ARNOLD, then one of the editors of that
paper; afterwards one of the founders, and
now a Curator, of the Georgia Historical Society.—*The Committee.*]

MR. WILDE AND "MY LIFE IS LIKE THE SUM-
MER ROSE."— On the 26th of August last, at
the request of several of our subscribers, we
published in the Georgian an article from the
New-York Weekly Register and Catholic Diary,
accusing Mr. Wilde of plagiarizing this cele-
brated little sonnet from the Irish poet O'Kelly.
In complying with the request of our subscribers, who believed the accusation to be true,
we observed : "We trust that the correspondent
of the 'Diary' is mistaken;" and further observed, in relation to settling the point : "It is
a dispute, however, which the Fair may more
appropriately settle. We hope, however, all
contests may be conducted in verse, and no
sharper weapons used than the plumes of the

eagle dipped in the fragrant attar of roses."
It is evident, from this language, what we
thought of the charge; and we only awaited a
denial from Mr. Wilde to give it a place in
our columns.

Mr. Wilde did not deny the charge of the
correspondent of the "Diary," and it gradually
traveled the round of the newspapers. Since
that time, we have come into possession of the
following facts, which will vindicate Mr. Wilde
against the charge of having plagiarized from
O'Kelly, (*who was alive at the visit of George 4th
to Ireland.*)

As long ago as 1822, a gentleman of this city
sent a copy of Mr. Wilde's "Summer Rose" to
Scotland, with a view to publication with
some poems from the pen of the late Denison,
in a literary periodical then publishing in
Greenock, entitled the "Coronal." The piece
of Mr. Wilde was actually published in Glasgow, Scotland, in a small volume of poems
entitled the "Columbian Lyre," which volume
is now lying before us. The gentleman who

9

communicates this, says that he has every reason
to believe that Mr. Mennons, the editor of the
"Coronal," published Mr. Wilde's fugitive in
the Greenock Advertiser, of which he was also
editor.   In the same volume, there also appears
an *answer* to the Summer Rose, by a lady of
Baltimore.

One of the evidences of the plagiarism offered
by the correspondent of the "Diary" was, that,
in the same volume in which O'Kelly's piece
was published, there was an answer to it by
Mr. J. O'Leary, of Cork.

So much for the charge of plagiarism from
the Irish Bard.

In relation to Alcæus, whom the editor of the
North American Magazine, Mr. Sumner Lincoln
Fairfield, ignorantly terms "one of the sweetest
of all the *erotic* bards of ancient Greece," when
every school-boy knows, that, although he was
in love with Sappho, his reputation arose from
lyric poetry, the truth is as follows :

Soon after the appearance of the article from
the "Diary," in our columns, a friend received

an anonymous letter, enclosing a copy of Greek
and Latin verses purporting to be the source
from which Wilde and O'Kelly had drawn their
inspiration, which the writer said he had found
among the fragments of ALCÆUS. They were
shown to us, and our friend and ourselves agreed
that it was a clever piece of *mystification;* and,
but for the want of Greek type, they should
have then appeared in our columns, not with
the remotest idea of injuring Mr. Wilde, but
as a harmless piece of mystification; a tub to
literary *minnows* who think themselves *whales.*

The whole circumstance had passed out of
our mind, until an article in the Globe, of the
18th inst., apprised us that the verses in question had been published in the North American
Magazine as a real and true Greek original, and
that their publication and the indorsement by
the learned Theban of the Magazine had excited
warm feelings on the part of Mr. Wilde's friends.

Passing by the illiberal charge made by the
National Intelligencer about the inability of *any
one* of the Jackson party to translate English

into Latin or Greek, we beg to disabuse that print of its delusion about its being "the work of some learned Whig to hoax the Globe." We *believe*, for we did not see them written, that the Greek and Latin verses in question were written by neither " whig " nor " tory "—without the design of traducing Mr. Wilde, or hoaxing the Globe in particular—but merely as a *jeu d'esprit*.

We are extremely sorry that we did not ask for a copy of them ; but we recollect well that the closeness of the translation alone caused us to say it was a clever hoax. We had no idea, neither do we believe had the author, that a clever hoax would have seriously invalidated the claim of Mr. Wilde to originality. The editor of the Magazine says : "This fragment, with the Latin translation, was transmitted from Georgia to our friend Dr. Bartlett, of the New-York Albion, and by him transferred to us for publication."

We have seen nothing to change our opinion of the claim of Mr. Wilde to originality, in relation to the verses commencing, "My life is like the summer rose."

Much as we differ from Mr. Wilde, on political points, we take great pleasure in expressing our warm admiration of him as a man of taste, genius, and classical attainments.

In concluding this volume, the Committee beg to say they deem it unnecessary to add anything, of their own, in praise of the poetic, chaste, and melodious verses of Mr. Wilde —

"THE LAMENT OF THE CAPTIVE;" or, as better known, "The Summer Rose." Ever since its first appearance, the little poem has won the admiration of all lovers of the beautiful in art. Its highest praise is, perhaps, to be found in the unwillingness of any one to yield gracefully the palm to Mr. Wilde. Hear what a genuine critic says.

Hon. GEORGE P. MARSH, in his "Lectures on the English Language," discussing the question of "imitative words," that is, words which

call up "resemblance between the sound and
the sense," observes, at page 570 :

"I know, however, in the whole range of
imitative verse, no line superior, perhaps I
should say none equal, to that in Wilde's cele-
brated nameless poem :

> Yet, as if grieving to efface
> All vestige of the human race,
> *On that lone shore loud moans the sea.*

Here the employment of monosyllables, of
long vowels and liquids, without harsh conso-
nantal sounds, together with the significance of
the words themselves, gives to the verse a force
of expression seldom if ever surpassed."